The SPACE ROCK Mystery

by Lydia Lukidis
illustrated by Shirley Ng-Benitez

Kane Press
New York

For my loving parents George and Christine Lukidis, who have supported me unconditionally throughout the years—L.L.

To Kimi, Sharon, and the beautiful islands and people of Hawaii—S.N.B.

Acknowledgements: Our thanks to Caitlin Coe, Science Educator, and to Rebeka Eston Salemi, Kindergarten Teacher, Lincoln School, Lincoln, MA, for helping us make this book as accurate as possible. Special thanks to Meagan Branday Susi for providing the activities in the back of this book.

Library of Congress Cataloging-in-Publication Data

Names: Lukidis, Lydia, author. | Ng-Benitez, Shirley, illustrator.
Title: The space rock mystery / by Lydia Lukidis ; illustrated by Shirley Ng-Benitez.
Description: New York : Kane Press, 2018. | Series: Science solves it! | Summary: Hawaiian siblings Leia and Kaleo learn about rocks and minerals when Kaleo finds a strange-looking rock on the beach. Includes science activities.
Identifiers: LCCN 2017046388 (print) | LCCN 2017015168 (ebook) | ISBN 9781635920062 (ebook) | ISBN 9781635920055 (pbk. : alk. paper)
Subjects: | CYAC: Rocks--Fiction. | Hawaii--Fiction.
Classification: LCC PZ7.1.L845 (print) | LCC PZ7.1.L845 Sp 2018 (ebook) | DDC [E]--dc23
LC record available at https://lccn.loc.gov/2017046388

10 9 8 7 6 5 4 3 2 1

First published in the United States of America in 2018 by Kane Press, Inc.
Printed in China

Science Solves It! is a registered trademark of Kane Press, Inc.

Book Design: Michelle Martinez

Visit us online at www.kanepress.com

Like us on Facebook
facebook.com/kanepress

Follow us on Twitter
@KanePress

"Please, pretty please!" Kaleo begged. "Can you come hunt for treasure with me?"

Leia laughed. "Treasure? You can't be serious!"

"Just for a teeny bit? I saw a shooting star last night," Kaleo said. "I think it landed somewhere on the beach."

"Oh, all right," Leia sighed. Going for a short walk was better than listening to her brother whine.

The two made their way to the beach. Kaleo was excited. He picked up every rock he saw.

Rocks come in all shapes, colors, and sizes! All rocks are made up of **minerals**, which are solid materials that are found in nature. Some examples of minerals are gold and lead.

Rock　　　　　　　**Mineral**

"Hey, look at this one!" Kaleo said. He shoved a shiny black rock right up to her face.

"Um, it's just a rock," Leia said.

"But look how cool it is!" He held it up to the light. It had huge craters. There were a bunch of glittering green crystals sticking out.

"This rock is totally from outer space," said Kaleo.

"No way!" said Leia.

"*Yes* way! It probably fell from the shooting star."

Kaleo talked about his new space rock for the rest of the afternoon.

The next day, Leia and
Kaleo went to the park
with their grandmother. They
called her Tutu, a Hawaiian name
for Grandma.

Leia played on the swings. Then she spotted
a big group of kids. They were gathering around
something. Leia made her way to the middle.
Right there at the center of all the action was
her brother.

"Step right up, folks!" Kaleo said. "Want to touch a REAL space rock?"

"What do you think you're doing?" Leia asked.

"I'm sharing the most special thing that ever happened to me," he said. "It's not every day you find a space rock!"

"Okay, that's it," Leia said. She dragged Kaleo over to Tutu.

"Tutu! Kaleo thinks he found a space rock. Can you please tell him it's not real?"

"Well," Tutu replied. "I need to see the rock first!"

Kaleo handed it over. Tutu examined it.

"This sure looks like a special rock," she said.

"Told you!" said Kaleo.

But Tutu wasn't sure. She suggested they visit her friend Mr. Kahale.

"Who's Mr. Kahale?" Leia asked.

"He's an expert on rocks and minerals," Tutu said. "He's very smart. He used to fly jets. And he was in the space program."

"Cool," Kaleo said. "Let's go now!"

A scientist who studies rocks is called a **geologist**.

When they got to Mr. Kahale's house, Leia raised
her hand to knock on the door. It popped open.

"Aloha!" sang Mr. Kahale.
He wore purple shorts and
a Hawaiian shirt. He also
wore a strange helmet on
his head. Leia gave Tutu a
"this-is-your-expert?" look.

Mr. Kahale grinned.
"Come on in!"

They sat down on a bright yellow couch. It looked like a banana.

"So. To what do I owe this most awesome visit?" he asked.

Kaleo plopped his rock onto the table. "Is this from outer space?"

Before anyone could speak, Leia cried out, "This is silly! It's just a rock."

Mr. Kahale gasped. "*Just* a rock? Did you know that every rock has a story, my dear? Rocks come in almost every color, size, and shape you can imagine. *Just a rock*, she says!"

He brought out a huge box full of rocks. Some were sparkly. Some were dull. Some were smooth and some were pointy. Leia picked up a rock with a wiggly pattern.

"The rock you're holding was formed from other rocks," Mr. Kahale said. "Deep inside the Earth there was a ton of heat and pressure. The rocks down there were squashed, stretched, and twisted until—*TA-DA!*—they made a new rock."

Leia's eyes widened as she ran her fingers over the rock.

Rocks that are formed out of other rocks because of heat and pressure are called **metamorphic**.

Next Mr. Kahale pointed at a brown rock. It had lots of speckles and spots.

"Other rocks take millions of years to form," he said. "Imagine a bunch of pebbles and sand. Over the years, they pile up. They harden and form solid rocks."

Layers of sand, mud, and pebbles that squash together into solid rock are called **sedimentary**. Sedimentary rocks are often formed in rivers, seas, and deserts.

Rocks made out of hot molten rock from inside the Earth are called **igneous**. Igneous rocks sometimes sparkle with crystals.

COOLING

Mr. Kahale picked up a third rock. It was black with holes in it. He put it in Leia's palm.

"And did you know that some rocks are made from liquid?" he said. "Inside the Earth, rock can heat up so much that it melts. When it cools down, it gets hard. Then, presto! It becomes a solid rock."

"But there are no space rocks, right?" Leia asked.

"Of course there are!" said Mr. Kahale. "Those are meteorites. They're chunks of rock or metal that fall from space. Most burn up before they hit the ground. But some make it to Earth."

When tiny rocks in space enter Earth's atmosphere, they burn up and create **meteors**. Sometimes you can see their trails of light in the night sky.

If any part of the rock survives burning up and lands on Earth, it is called a **meteorite**.

Kaleo was bouncing on his toes. "So what about my rock?"

Mr. Kahale grabbed a pair of funny looking goggles. He examined the rock.

"Nope," he finally said. "Sorry, but this rock is not from outer space."

Kaleo's shoulders slumped.

Mr. Kahale smiled. "Oh, but it's still a special rock!"

"Why?" Leia asked.

"Now that's the mystery!" he said. "To solve it, the three of you must come on an adventure. Meet me tomorrow at the town center. Be there at six in the evening. And wear running shoes."

Mr. Kahale stood up. "Now please excuse me. I have to get back to my anti-gravity water experiment!"

Then he disappeared down the hallway.

Leia had to admit Mr. Kahale sure knew a lot about rocks. Her mind began to race. She wondered what this adventure could be.

The next day, they went to the town center with Tutu. Mr. Kahale was waiting for them. They all hopped into his car. Leia asked where they were going.

"You'll see!" Mr. Kahale said.

When the car stopped, Leia looked out
the window. They were at the bottom of a
mountain.

"Time for a hike!" Mr. Kahale sang.

Leia and Kaleo kept asking where they were
going. Mr. Kahale just smiled. After an hour of
hiking, they reached the top.

"Surprise!" Mr. Kahale said. "It's a volcano! Hawaii has a number of them. But this one is not popular. I come here sometimes, to explore."

Leia gulped. "Volcano?"

"Not to worry," Mr. Kahale said. "It's not active. That means it won't erupt anymore."

Kaleo looked confused. "This volcano is cool and all. But what does it have to do with my rock?"

Just then, Leia saw a crystal glittering in the sun. She picked it up. It looked just like Kaleo's rock.

"Hey, it's the same rock as yours," she said. "Wait a minute. Are these volcano rocks?"

Some igneous rocks are made below the surface of the earth. But some are made above it—from a volcano's lava! Lava is formed when molten rock reaches the surface of the Earth.

"Bingo!" Mr. Kahale said. "Imagine an active volcano. *BOOM!* It erupts! Lava spurts out. When the lava cools down, volcanic rocks form."

"So we solved the mystery!" Leia said.

Mr. Kahale grinned.

"I'm glad," said Kaleo. "I don't mind that my rock isn't from outer space."

"You *don't?*" Leia asked.

Kaleo shook his head. "Volcanic rocks are way cooler!"

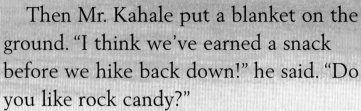

Then Mr. Kahale put a blanket on the ground. "I think we've earned a snack before we hike back down!" he said. "Do you like rock candy?"

The blue sky slowly turned pink.

Leia nudged her brother. "Look!" A shooting star zoomed high above them.

"Wow, a meteor!" Kaleo said.

When they finished their snack, Mr. Kahale and Tutu folded up the blanket. They all hiked back down the volcano.

Kaleo yawned as he climbed into the car. His face looked sleepy but happy. "Leia?" he asked. "Will you hunt for treasure with me tomorrow?"

Leia smiled. "Of course I will." She looked out at the stars. "And together, I think we can find a real space rock!"

I can classify!

Me too!

THINK LIKE A SCIENTIST

Leia and Kaleo think like scientists—and so can you!

A good scientist sorts objects by identifying their similarities and differences. Leia and Kaleo learned how rocks are classified into three different categories—sedimentary, metamorphic, and igneous—based on how the rocks were formed.

Look Back

- Look back to pages 5–6. Why did Kaleo think the rock had fallen from space?
- On page 14, what did Mr. Kahale mean when he said, "Every rock has a story?"
- On page 28, how did Kaleo feel after he found out where his rock came from?

Try This!

Gather a collection of rocks from various locations. Observe the rocks. Use a Venn diagram to classify them by attributes (size, color, texture, shape). Label the circles of the Venn diagram with attributes from different categories. For example, **small**, **gray**, **smooth**. Or **large**, **multicolored**, **rough**.

What similarities and differences do you see?

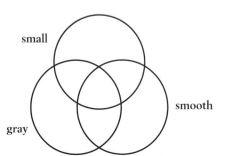

small

smooth

gray